EMOTES!®

THE CREATION

When the emotions of all Internet users came together, a new super-energy was created. This energy split into unique beings, each of which represents a different emotion. They are the Emotes!

A-NET
(THE MENTOR)

SUPER
(THE CONFIDENT)

ABASH
(THE EMBARRASSED)

JOI
(THE EXCITED)

YAWNI
(THE BORED)

ICK
(THE DISGUSTED)

MIXY
(THE CONFUSED)

BUBBA
(THE HAPPY)

CANT
(THE FRUSTRATED)

JUMPI
(THE SHOCKED)

BOOM
(THE ANGRY)

DRAIN
(THE EXHAUSTED)

IMP
(THE MISCHIEVOUS)

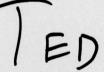

Cant Loses His Cool

By Matt Casper and Ted Dorsey

Evergrow Ltd.

Hong Kong — Los Angeles

www.Emotes.com

ISBN 13: 978-988-17342-2-8

Printed in China

Cant, Bubba, and Yawni were hanging out, watching a
telescreen program about pulsar beasts. Pulsar beasts are scary
creatures with big red eyes, snarly mouths, and angry howls.

Yawni yawned. "This is *soooo* boring. How could anyone be scared of a pulsar beast?"

Bubba laughed, but Cant quickly changed the channel. Pulsar beasts frightened him.

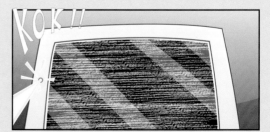

Suddenly, the telescreen filled with lots of colors and digital fireworks. "iiiiiiIIIIIIIIT's HERE!" cried a giant robotron.

The robotron was holding an ordinary-looking rubber ball. "The Amazingly-Fabulous-Awesomely-Spectacular Digiball goes on sale tomorrow morning at Quasar's Toy Store. Be there or be square!"

That's amazing!

Can't jumped to his feet and switched off the telescreen.

"Tomorrow morning?! Tomorrow will be here before we know it!"
he cried, pushing his friends out the door.

That night, Cant decided to go to bed extra early. He wanted to be the first in line the next morning to get a new Amazingly-Fabulous-Awesomely-Spectacular Digiball. He didn't care what made it so amazing, fabulous, and spectacular. He just knew he wanted one.

Very early the next morning, Cant's Alarmatron3000 went off. An enormous trumpet blogger popped out of the top and blared, "BLUUURGH!" Cant leaped out of bed and headed for the door.

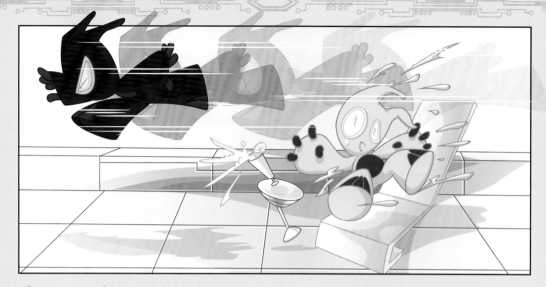

Cant ran faster than he had ever run before. He jumped over Drain, who was taking a nap in the middle of the cyber-pong courts.

He sped past Jumpi, who was tending to his pixel flower garden.

As Cant turned the corner of Microbyte Avenue, he saw something that made him stop in his tracks.

A big group of Emotes was lined up outside Quasar's Toy Store. Cant would not be the first in line. In fact, he would be the very *last* in line.

All the other Emotes were buzzing about the Digiball, but Cant was very quiet. He didn't feel like talking at all.

Suddenly the door to Quasar's flew open and the robotron appeared. "Come and get 'em!" it shouted.

As the line of Emotes moved forward, Cant felt his excitement return.

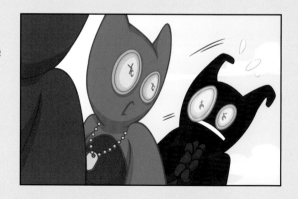

Cant and the other Emotes began making plans to use their Digiballs. They decided to play Digiballooza together that afternoon.

Cant no longer cared that he was last in line. He was having too much fun with his Emote friends.

Suddenly, there was a flash of light and the store's door slammed shut. The robotron hung a neon sign above the door: SORRY, ALL SOLD OUT.

The other Emotes ran out of Quasar's, laughing and throwing their new Digiballs high into the air.

Cant's face begin to twitch. His throat tightened. He began to shake his fists and stomp his feet.

One by one, the other Emotes noticed Cant shimmying and shaking. They all stopped and stared.

"NOOOOOOOOOOOOOOOOOOOO!" Cant cried.

The Emotes scattered in every direction, covering their ears as they raced away. A small orbaprobe dropped its fiber optics and quickly took off.

"It's just not fair!" Cant shouted over and over again.

Cant felt powerless. He tried to stop screaming, but he couldn't. He was so upset that he didn't even notice A-Net approaching him.

A-Net stopped directly in front of Cant and made a large refecto-viewer appear.

Can you see yourself clearly?

Cant fell silent. He was looking at himself, and he did not like what he saw. He looked every bit as scary as the pulsar beast he had seen on the telescreen the night before.

"You are very frustrated right now. It's okay. Just take a few deep breaths and close your eyes," said A-Net.

Cant obeyed. Then he listened closely to what A-Net had to say.

"I want you to think of things that you like," A-Net began. "Picture them in your mind and let your imagination run free."

Cant began to think about marshmallow pods and infrared cakes. He imagined himself flying way up high in the Eosphere. Slowly, he began to cool down.

When Cant opened his eyes, he saw Bubba standing next to A-Net. They were both smiling at him.

"Tell me how you're feeling," Bubba said.

Cant explained how excited he had been about the Digiball, and how disappointed he was that he couldn't have one. He put his feelings into words like *frustrated*, *angry*, *sad*, and *confused*.

Bubba listened closely to everything that Cant said. Then he gave his friend a great big hug. That made Cant feel much better.

"It's okay to be frustrated and disappointed sometimes," said Bubba. "It happens to everyone. The secret is to put your feelings into words, not tantrums. Tantrums just make you feel worse."

"You've got that right," said Cant, laughing. "I felt like a pulsar beast who skipped breakfast. Let's get out of here!"

Bubba and Cant headed to Macro's, their favorite restaurant, where they shared a giant infrared cake. Soon Cant had forgotten all about the Digiball. He was just happy to be with his good friend Bubba.

THE END

CANT TALKS ABOUT TANTRUMS:

Sometimes I throw a tantrum when I'm frustrated. It feels like I'm spinning around and around and I can't make the spinning stop. Everyone feels this way every now and again. When I really want something and can't have it, I get frustrated and really angry.

Sometimes the frustration is so strong that it's hard to express in words. That's when my tantrums happen.

The problem with tantrums is that they don't work. In fact, tantrums make me feel even worse. I've learned that tantrums are not a good way to show someone how I'm feeling.

Talking about how I'm feeling is always better than having a tantrum.

"WHEN I FEEL FRUSTRATED, WHAT CAN I DO?"

◉ First, I take a deep breath to help me chill out. Maybe even a couple of deep breaths, if I'm really fired up.

◉ I try and think about the feelings I'm having and find words that describe them. I even say these words out loud to myself or someone else. I do a "check-in" with myself and ask, "Hey dude, are you having a tantrum?" When I put my feelings into words, it becomes easier for me to control them.

◉ When I'm beginning to feel frustrated, it calms me down to think about some of my favorite things. I think about my friends and how much fun we have together. Sometimes doing something that I like to do can help me cool down, too, like taking a walk or playing a game of cyber-pong.

◉ Remember that it is totally normal and okay to feel frustrated or confused. People of all ages feel this way sometimes.

◉ Being frustrated is nothing to be ashamed of. Talking about your frustration is something to be proud of!

ABOUT THE AUTHORS:

Matt Casper, M.A., MFT. Matt is a licensed Marriage and Family Therapist. He graduated from Duke University, where he studied psychology, religion, and film. He received his master's degree in Marriage and Family Therapy from the California Graduate Institute of Professional Psychology and Psychoanalysis. Matt currently lives in Los Angeles, where he works with people of all ages to help them identify, understand, and express their emotions.

Ted Dorsey is a writer and independent educator living in Los Angeles, California. A graduate of Princeton University, he has written for the stage, film, and television.

EMOTES!

EMOTES!
Abash and the Cyber-Bully
Matt Casper and Ted Dorsey

EMOTES!
Cant Loses His Cool

EMOTES!
Jumpi Goes to Camp
Matt Casper and Ted Dorsey

EMOTES!
Drain and the Mystery of Sleep
Matt Casper and Ted Dorsey

Joi's Cybercoaster Adventure
Matt Casper and Ted Dorsey

EMOTES!
Super and Perfecto
Matt Casper and Ted Dorsey

EMOTES!
Imp and the Fib Invasion
Matt Casper and Ted Dorsey

EMOTES!
Ick and the Emotastone
Matt Casper and Ted Dorsey

Yawni and the Perspecto-Goggles
Matt Casper and Ted Dorsey

Boom the Anger Tamer
Matt Casper and Ted Dorsey

Bubba Under Pressure
Matt Casper and Ted Dorsey

EMOTES!

EMOTES!
Mixy's Quest
Matt Casper and Ted Dorsey

AND MANY MORE!

www.Emotes.com
©Evergrow Ltd.